SEDNA
An Eskimo Myth

Adapted and illustrated by
Beverly Brodsky McDermott

The Viking Press New York

FIRST EDITION.

Copyright © 1975 by Beverly Brodsky McDermott. All rights reserved. First published in 1975 by The Viking Press, Inc., 625 Madison Avenue, New York, N.Y. 10022. Published simultaneously in Canada by The Macmillan Company of Canada Limited. Printed in U.S.A. 1 2 3 4 5 79 78 77 76 75

Library of Congress Cataloging in Publication Data
McDermott, Beverly Brodsky   Sedna: an Eskimo myth.   Bibliography: p.
Summary: Sedna, mother of all sea animals, tells the story of her life and helps the starving Inuit.
1. Eskimos—Legends.   2. Indians of North America—Legends.   [1. Eskimos—Legends]   I. Title.   E99.E7B77
398.2'454 [E]   75–4979   ISBN 0–670–63165–5

ABOUT THE AUTHOR

BEVERLY BRODSKY MCDERMOTT chose the Sedna myth, she says, because she was "impressed with the idea of a water spirit as a potent female symbol who controls the forces of nature. The Inuit conception of art is very special, too. It is not art for art's sake as we know it, but a function of daily life. Sometimes making an object so small that it fits in the palm of the hand, the Eskimo will carve a piece of ivory or wood until its hidden form emerges. Though our conception differs, we share a similar approach in that I work patiently, watching for colors to erupt and shapes to be released from the surface of the paper or canvas. I admire the way the Eskimo uses delicate linear detail and subtle, sensuous contours to bring the form to life."

Ms. McDermott is a graduate of Brooklyn College, where she studied painting under Ad Reinhardt. She is also the author and illustrator of *The Crystal Apple: A Russian Tale*. She and her husband make their home in the Hudson River Valley.

ABOUT THE BOOK

The art work for *Sedna* was done with pen and brush and black ink on paper and was preseparated. The display type is Albertus and the text type is Melior. The book was printed by offset, and is bound in cloth over boards. The binding is reinforced and side-sewn.

BIBLIOGRAPHY

Carpenter, Edmund. *Eskimo Realities*. New York: Holt, Rinehart, and Winston, 1973.
Collins, Henry B., Frederica De Laguna, Edmund Carpenter, and Peter Stone. *The Far North: 2000 Years of American Eskimo and Indian Art*. Washington: The National Gallery of Art, 1973.
Rasmussen, Knud. *The People of the Polar North*. London: Kegan Paul, Trench, Trubner & Company, 1908.
Thompson, Stith. *Tales of North American Indians*. Bloomington and London: Indiana University Press, 1968.
Wherry, Joseph H. *Indian Masks and Myths of the West*. New York: Funk and Wagnall, 1969.

SEDNA

Winter's darkness cast
her shadow over the arctic plain.
The Inuit were hungry and sick.
They longed to fill their stomachs
with the tender meat
of the seal and walrus.

Day after day the hunters
waited for Sedna,
the powerful sea spirit,
to release her animals.

The Inuit called to the Angakok
to work his special magic.
"Please help our people.
Ask the sea spirit to
send forth her gifts."

When the Angakok
chanted his magic song,
the earth trembled
and the sea churned.

As he listened to the troubled sea,
Sedna rose from the waves.
She ignored the pleas of the Angakok.
Instead she told a story
to the man of magic.

"When I was young and beautiful,
I was wooed by many men.
But I loved only one.
His song was so enchanting
that I agreed to become his wife.

"Much later I discovered
that he was a cunning spirit,
a sea bird who had transformed himself
into a man. To take on human shape,
he had shed his feathers
and removed his beak.

"We lived among the petrels, and their constant chatter was like the cries of a thousand winds. Oh, how frightened and confused I became.
I longed for the serenity of my village.

"My father shivered when he looked up
and saw the sky grow black.
Helpless against the fierce bird spirit,
he threw me into the icy waters.
I struggled to breathe
and clung to the boat.

"To save himself my father struck
at my hands.

"One day I left the cliff nest
and returned to my people.
I begged them to save me.

"But the bird spirit was too powerful.
He made the dogs howl and caused
huge waves to swallow the huts.
Many people and animals died.

"'You must return Sedna to me,'
the bird spirit warned. But my
father did not listen. We climbed
into an oomyak to escape. 'Return Sedna,'
demanded the petrel, once again.

"My fingers broke into little pieces
and fell into the sea.

"As I watched, I saw my fingers become
shiny seals, fat walruses, and great
whales. And so I became mother of
all sea beasts. Now I live beneath
the sea. I am a powerful spirit,"
she sighed, "but I am clumsy.
I cannot plait my hair nor
rid myself of its parasites."

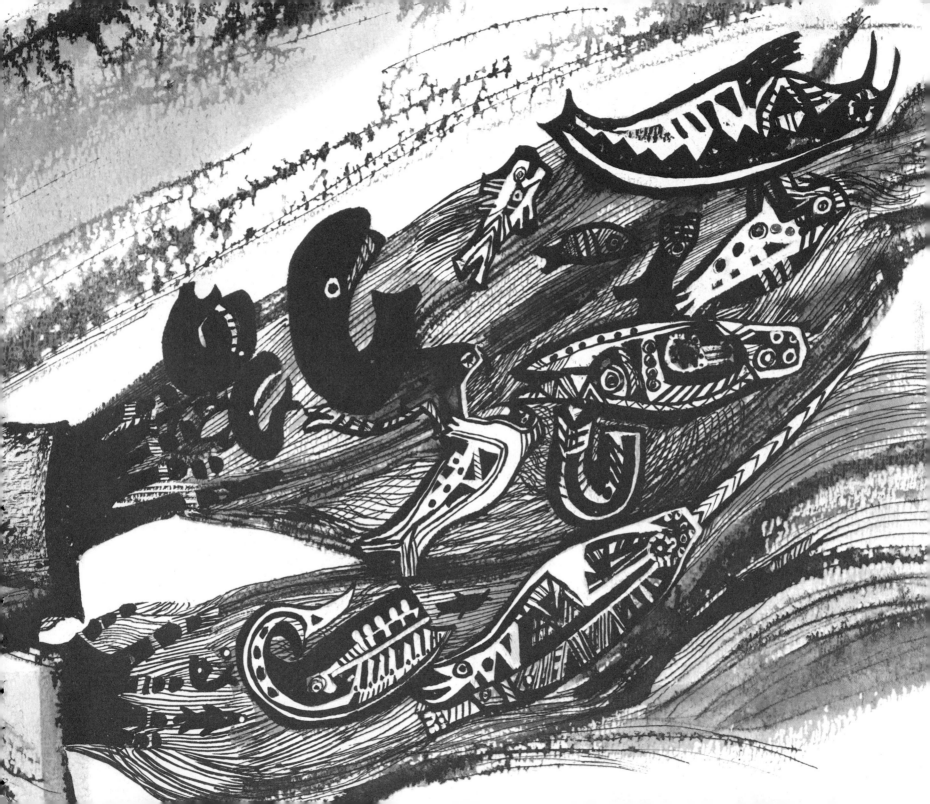

The Angakok was moved
by Sedna's sad story.
He knew what he must do.

Quickly he plunged
past the ice floes
and followed Sedna
to the bottom of the sea.

He found Sedna in a dark hut.
The entrance was guarded by a giant dog.
Sedna was covered with seaweed,
and little animals crawled in her hair.
In a bitter tone she demanded:
"Plait my hair and rid me
of these parasites."

The Angakok replied:
"Yes, I will do so.
But you must promise to send
your gifts of food to our people.
Drive the seal and walrus
toward us so that we may live!"

Sedna agreed.
She guided the seals up
through the breathing holes,
letting the hunters trap them.
The women prepared the seals
and cut off large chunks of meat
for the hungry people.
Joy came to the Inuit.
They gave thanks
before the great feast.

The sea was calm once more,
for the powerful mother
of all sea beasts was pleased.
She was grateful to the Angakok
for arranging her hair
and satisfied that the people
had shown respect for her bounty.

The Inuit know that
whenever there is
hunger and sickness
it is because the spirits
of the dead are unhappy.
The living must never forget them.